tiny giant:
NATE ARCHIBALD

Author

Jeff Greenfield

Photography

Heinz Kluetmeier
Bruce Curtis

 **RAINTREE EDITIONS**

Published by   **Raintree Editions**
                 A Division of Raintree Publishers Limited
                 Milwaukee, Wisconsin 53203

Distributed by   Childrens Press
                 1224 West Van Buren Street
                 Chicago, Illinois 60607

Library of Congress Cataloging in Publication Data

Greenfield, Jeff.
  Tiny giant.

  SUMMARY: A biography of professional basketball's
shortest man, who had to fight for recognition.
  1. Archibald, Nate, 1948-   —Juvenile literature.
2. Basketball—Juvenile literature. [1. Archibald, Nate,
1948-   2. Basketball—Biography]
I. Curtis, Bruce. II. Kluetmeier, Heinz. III. Title.
GV884.A7G74   796.32'3'0924 [B] [92]   75-42035
ISBN 0-8172-0125-4
ISBN 0-8172-0124-6 lib. bdg.

Contents

1

Tiny Giant

Suppose you were at a basketball game, and your home town team was playing the Kansas City Kings. If you didn't follow professional basketball, you might wonder about that guy leading the Kings onto the court. He looks like a high school kid. He's a foot shorter than the other players; he's skinny; his wide eyes make him look years younger than anyone else on the court. Why are they letting him warm up with the real players? Is he their mascot? The owner's son? Did he win some sort of "King for a Day" contest?

Then the game would start. And suddenly you'd see very clearly what that "kid" was doing on the basketball court. You'd see him take the ball down the court, run around his opponent, leap high into the air, shift the ball from his left hand to his right in mid-air, and lay the ball into the basket. A moment later you might see him drive to the basket again; only this time, as the other team put two of their men on him, he'd stop almost in mid-flight to pass the ball to an open teammate for an easy score. The next time, the other team might retreat a few steps, waiting to stop this "kid" before he took off again. Only this time, he'd pull up and shoot the ball from 15 or 20 feet away. And if he played this game the way he plays most, you'd see a whole bagful of shots, moves, and passes that would have you off your seat in amazement.

4

For this is no mascot, no underage player along for kicks. This is Nate ("Tiny") Archibald, one of the most famous superstars of professional basketball. Though he is only 26 years old, he is already considered one of the two or three best guards in the NBA, and is building a record which may mark him as one of the best ever to play the game.

At six feet, 160 pounds, Nate is one of the smallest players in the league. His nickname, "Tiny," which he has had since he was a child, seems very accurate when you compare him to other players in the league.

But "Tiny" has already accomplished what no one else, big or little, has ever done in the NBA's history: He has, for an entire season, led the league in both scoring *and* assists. That is almost impossible to do. It means you've both set up more baskets than anyone else in the league, and scored more points than anyone else. It's something like leading the National Football League in passing and pass

catching, or leading the major baseball league in pitching and hitting.

"Tiny" Archibald has proven what lots of fans, and some coaches, forget: that in a big man's game, there is always room for the small player who has speed, shooting and passing ability, and guts. By those standards, Tiny is one of the biggest men in basketball today.

But if you just watched Nate Archibald on the court, you would have learned only half the story of this remarkable man. Just as impressive is the story of how he got there: where he came from, how he struggled out of poverty, how he was helped to keep his ambition alive, and how today Tiny Archibald, one of the best-paid and most famous athletes in America, spends almost all of his spare time working with kids who live the way he used to.

Growing Up Poor

Most of us learn in school that America is the richest nation in the world. It is. But in this richest of nations there are still millions of poor people. Some of them live in tarpaper shacks along dirt roads far up in the hills and down in the valleys, far from towns and cities. Some of them are old, too sick or weak to work, living on charity that is never enough to buy them hot meals or good clothes. And others live in our biggest cities, crowded together because they cannot afford anything better, living in apartments with peeling paint, broken plumbing, rats and cockroaches.

Nate Archibald was one of these poor people. He was born in 1949 in Harlem, a New York black ghetto. When he was very young his family moved to a public housing project in the South Bronx, another ghetto even poorer and more dangerous than Harlem. He and his six brothers and sisters lived in a three-room apartment. "The four boys shared one room; three girls shared another room," he remembers. "We were on welfare at that time, and everything was grim and looked grim."

When Tiny was still a child, his father left home, and his mother was left alone to support the children. She worked as a salesclerk in Alexander's Department Store up in the Bronx. She struggled to keep her children out of trouble;

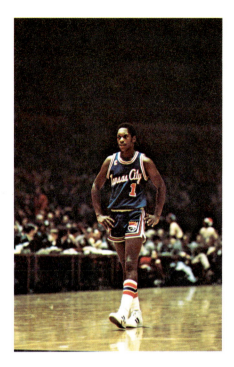

trouble was very easy to find in this kind of neighborhood. It was hard. Archibald remembers hearing his mother crying herself to sleep, alone, late at night. There was money to worry about, of course, and the burden of holding down a job and being the only parent for seven children. But there was something even more serious to worry about: the epidemic of drugs that was threatening young people all over the poorer neighborhoods of New York. Tiny remembers it all too well:

"It was in the streets of the South Bronx, and in the streets of Manhattan," he says. "I was born over at 118th Street, and my grandmother was still living there when I was growing up, so I would visit her there from time to time. People were just laying in the streets; either they had O.D.ed (took so much dope that they passed out or even died), or they were just high. If people don't believe it, they can go *now* to 116th Street or 118th Street, and see these people there. I'm not saying everybody's on drugs, but they're hanging out, they're on the streets, and it's nothing really — they're just there."

It is like that in a poor neighborhood. There are many families with only one parent, and many other families where there is no work for either the mother or the father. There may be a welfare check, or occasional money from odd jobs. But there is no security, and few examples of people holding jobs that children might want to have when they grow up. Instead, there are people hanging around on street corners with nothing to do, and there is a deep feeling that any escape from life is welcome — even if it comes from a pill or white powder injected into your veins. For those who try drugs when they are still teenagers, life may become a series of crimes committed to find money for drugs. It may become a revolving door — in and out of detention centers and jails. It may be over at 16 or 18, in a violent exchange of gunfire, or from a body ruined by drugs. (When Tiny was practicing one day with his high school team, a teammate collapsed of a drug over-dose. "He died right there on the court," says Archibald.)

Fortunately, for Tiny Archibald and for other youngsters, there is another kind of escape from the reality of life in the ghetto. It does not cost money, it is legal, and it is healthy, not poisonous. That escape is basketball. For a poor child in the city, basketball is by far the most popular sport. A child's family may be too poor to buy a tennis racket, a hockey stick, even a baseball glove. But there is an asphalt basketball court, with backboard and rim, in every schoolyard in the city, and somewhere somebody can find a ball. So just about any time of day or night, and just about any time of year, you'll see kids running, leaping, shooting, fighting for rebounds. "I don't care what anybody says," Archibald insists, "New York is the basketball capital of the world." For a lot of poor kids, basketball means a few hours of fun; a chance to test their talents against those of their friends and neighbors. For many, it's a dream of something to do with their lives.

That's how it was for Tiny. But he also had a break. He met up with a man who taught him to care — not just about basketball, but about making something of his own life. It's because of that man, who helped Tiny Archibald out of the ghetto and into the world of success, that Tiny himself spends so much of his life in the same kind of work. The man's name is Floyd Lane.

Somebody Special

Tiny Archibald is right; New York is the basketball capital of the world. But the fact of poverty and ghetto life means that there are many different levels of basketball. Just a short subway ride away from the South Bronx is Madison Square Garden, probably the most famous basketball arena in the world. It's the home of the New York Knickerbockers, and the site of some of the greatest professional and college basketball games in sports history. You would think that a child like Archibald, playing basketball so many hours of so many days, would have spent much of his time there. But the truth is that until Tiny was a player himself, he never set foot inside Madison Square Garden.

"Sure it was a subway ride away," he says, "but the tickets were $7, $8. I couldn't get in the door."

So Archibald played his basketball on the playgrounds of the South Bronx, and in the community center at his elementary school, P.S. 18, up on Morris Avenue and 143rd Street. It was right next to the projects where he and his family lived. Tiny would play every day after school from three to five, then go home for dinner, and then play some more from seven until nine. It was there that he met the community center's director, Floyd Lane.

Floyd had been a basketball star himself, a star backcourt

man on the City College of New York team that had won
the National Invitational Tournament in 1950. But a year later,
the CCNY team was hit by a scandal. Gamblers had been
paying some of the players to score fewer points than
they could have, so that the gamblers could win bets on
what the final scores would be. The scandal ruined many of
the players. They dropped out of basketball. Floyd Lane,
however, began to devote himself to working with New York
City kids. He used basketball to get them interested,
and then worked with them to continue their educations. In
1963, he was running the community center at P.S. 18,
where Nate Archibald was going to school.

"He was just one of the youngsters," Floyd says today.
(Lane is now the basketball coach at CCNY.) "There was
nothing special about his talent, you didn't notice anything of
any particular specialty. He was a good little player who
knew his way around the court pretty well."

But Tiny remembers how Floyd Lane got him involved in basketball competitions.

"I started with the Ray Felix Tournament out on Long Island," he says. "Ray Felix was an ex-pro who tried to organize basketball for kids. There was nothing like it in the city, so we used to go all the way out to Elmhurst by subway and train. It took two hours. Then some ex-athletes who called themselves the Courtsmen started to put together a citywide tournament for kids in New York, and I used to play in those every summer. And when I was in high school, I started to coach the 'biddies' — the littler kids."

Even more important was what Floyd Lane told Tiny about his life off the basketball court.

"Playing pro ball is in every youngster's mind," Tiny says, "but it's just a dream; it wasn't something I had in my mind that I must do. It was that someday I'd like to be there.

"But Floyd didn't emphasize that; he emphasized more of going to school, trying to make your junior high school team, going to high school, trying to make your high school team, and doing something with your time. A lot of youngsters go to school from nine to three, and they have so much time other than that to do something with, and most of them just don't do anything."

Tiny knew a lot of kids who didn't do anything. "And you know what they're doing now? The same thing as when I left them. Nothing. They don't have a job, they're not going to school, they're just living from day to day. They get up, go outside, hang out, and come back, and that's their job. This was what Floyd was talking about."

Tiny almost didn't make his high school basketball team. He attended New York's DeWitt Clinton High School, an all-boys' school with 5,000 students. Obviously, Clinton had a lot of basketball talent to choose from. Tiny went out for the team, but got cut. Then Floyd Lane got involved.

"I went up to see the coach, whom I had known from high school, and I spoke to him, asking him to look Nate up. He said, 'Tell the youngster to come back.' I guess it was just that little bit of encouragement that got him to go back."

Basketball kept Tiny in school. Apart from his art classes, he was not all that involved with his studies. But he knew that the only way to stay eligible for his high school team was to do well in his classes. And the only possible way he could get to college was to build up a reputation as a good high school basketball player and win an athletic scholarship.

By his junior year, Archibald was a solid member of the DeWitt Clinton team, and by his senior year, he was good enough to get named to the All-City public school basketball team.

But already people were starting to ask questions, not about his talent, but about his size. He had proven that he was a smart, fast player with a kind of "sixth sense" for basketball, knowing when to shoot and when to pass, able to dribble and move the ball very quickly. But by the end of high school, the nickname Archibald had gotten from his father — they called his father "Tiny" even though he was six-feet-two — was being used as an accurate description of the six-foot player.

College recruiters surround a player like Wilt Chamberlain or Kareem Abdul-Jabbar from the time they're old enough to cross the street by themselves. Any good athlete who is also seven feet tall is a natural for college ball. Moses Malone, the six-foot-ten-inch Utah Stars player who went right from high school into pro ball, was offered more than 250 scholarships to play in college. It got so bad that Malone sometimes hid under the bed when he saw another college recruiter coming.

When you are a quick, small ballplayer, however, the recruiters do not come around so often. They wonder, quite naturally, how you will do against equally-talented players who are four or five inches taller. In big time basketball, many of the best guards — Walt Frazier, Phil Chenier, Jo Jo White, to name three — are both fast *and* tall. Someone like Tiny Archibald can easily get lost in a crowd.

While in high school, Tiny had been working in a super-market. He knew that if he didn't get an athletic scholarship, "I probably would never go to college anywhere." But once again, Floyd Lane got in touch with a friend of his. Tiny was given a scholarship to a junior college, Arizona Western in Yuma, Arizona.

It was quite a change. Archibald had never been out of the City of New York in his life — not even to New Jersey, which is just across the Hudson River.

"Going from New York to Yuma was like going to Mars," he remembers now. "The townspeople were very pleasant and all, but it was nothing like New York City. And the

20

school was all we had, because after you got from the airport to the town to the school, that was it. I remember asking the coach, 'Where's the city?' And he laughed and said, 'There isn't any.' ''

Archibald's basketball at Arizona Western was good enough to get him a scholarship to a regular four-year college, the University of Texas at El Paso. As far as learning basketball, it was an important step.

New York City playground basketball is a very fast, individual game. Players concentrate on their moves, their shots, scoring points against the man guarding them. It is not a totally team sport.

At UTEP (as the University of Texas at El Paso is called), Archibald was coached by Clem Haskins, who stressed a very different kind of game. The tempo was much slower; the offense was based not on outrunning the other team down the floor, but on working the ball to a free player for a good shot. As the ball-handling guard, Tiny was the "quarterback" of the team.

By the time he left college, Tiny knew two kinds of basketball — the fast, run-and-shoot New York playground style, and the slower "pattern offense" game that every team needs to score when it can't outrun the opponents down the court. He was ready for the professional draft.

Tiny's team was not famous enough to play on national television networks, so many fans and professional coaches had not heard too much about the young man. But, according to Rickie Sobers, a neighbor from the South Bronx and now a rookie with the Phoenix Suns, "Everybody knew that Tiny was going to make it in the pros." Tiny was a player with a reputation in New York, but not across the nation.

One coach who did know about Tiny was Bob Cousy of the Cincinnati Royals. Cousy himself was small, but he had been one of the great pro guards of all time, playing with the champion Boston Celtics of the 1950s and 1960s. Cousy liked Tiny's style, and obviously knew that a "little man" could be valuable. The Royals made Tiny a second round draft choice. Cousy figured they could sign him for about $30,000 a year.

Cousy knew that Archibald was good, but he didn't know just how good until he watched Tiny playing in a few All-Star games. In one game in Memphis, Tennessee, Archibald scored 28 points. A few days later in Indianapolis, he scored 38 points.

Because of that performance, Tiny was invited to an All-Star tournament in Hawaii, where he scored 122 points in three games, with an incredible 51 points in the last game.

As it happened, Cousy was talking to Tiny's college coach by phone when he found out how well Tiny had done in Hawaii. Cousy was amazed. But so was Haskins.

"I'm just as surprised as you guys," Haskins said. "He played for me for three years, and I never knew he could score like that."

So the Cincinnati Royals discovered that they had a fast guard who could handle the ball, pass it, and also score. Tiny Archibald wound up signing his first professional basketball contract, not for $30,000 a year, but for more than $150,000 a year. When he signed, this New York City ghetto kid had exactly 16 cents in his pockets.

Star to Superstar

Nate Archibald is not a flamboyant talker. He is not a braggart. But he *is* a man with a strong sense of his own ability. Many rookie players, particularly players without overwhelming size or strength, find it difficult to believe that they really belong on the same basketball court with players they were watching on TV just a few short years ago. But it didn't take Tiny long to realize that he belonged in the NBA.

"Everybody questions their ability, even if they're six-feet-ten," Archibald says. "You don't know if you're going to be a player or a superstar, and then after you get those first couple of games under your belt, you can guess where you stand. After my first game, I thought I played pretty well, and I said, 'Hmmmm, I might be here for awhile.' "

Archibald didn't have time to doubt himself anyway. The Cincinnati Royals were a weak team, and Archibald found himself in a starting position right away. But his first year did not bring him much recognition, partly because Cincinnati was a losing ball club, partly because big men tend to get more publicity than smaller men.

It was something that happened in his second year that turned Nate Archibald into a genuine star. Through the first

half of that season — 1971-'72 — Archibald had been playing first-rate ball. He had been scoring more than 20 points a game, passing brilliantly to teammates, and in general leading his team. But once again the Royals were losing more games than they won; once again it was the more celebrated players from the more successful teams who got the publicity. So when the voting for the NBA All-Star team was held in the middle of the year, Archibald did not make it.

"I made up my mind to make somebody pay for that," he said later. "I play only one way — fast and aggressive."

As it turned out, the rest of the league wound up paying. In the second half of the season, Tiny went crazy. With a dazzling assortment of shots, fakes, moves, passes, and all-around play, he began scoring points as though he were a pinball machine: 55 against Portland; 49 against New York. He wound up with a scoring average of 28 points

a game, second in the league only to Kareem Abdul-Jabbar, who is about 15 inches taller than Tiny.

In the next season, the Cincinnati Royals moved their location to become the Kansas City-Omaha Kings — and Nate Archibald moved to superstardom. Coach Cousy, seeing that his team could not make the playoffs, deliberately decided to turn Archibald into a high-scoring player, hoping that fans would pay to see a superstar, if not a super-team. He told Tiny to take over leadership of the team — to score as much as he could, remembering only to share the scoring once in awhile with his teammates. Tiny followed the strategy — right into the record books.

He scored more points than any other guard in NBA history — averaging 34 points a game, to lead the league in scoring. When you remember that players like Jabbar and Wilt Chamberlain score most of their points a few feet from the basket, this record is very impressive. A guard

plays away from the basket; he scores his points either with accuracy — shooting from 15 or 20 feet away — or by bringing the ball to the basket, fighting his way through much taller players. But Archibald *also* led the league in *assists,* averaging more than 11 a game. This means that apart from his own scoring, his passing directly accounted for 11 baskets — 22 points a game.

While an injury sidelined Archibald for most of the next season, he came back in 1974-'75 to demonstrate his talents again: He averaged 26.5 points a game (fourth best in the league) and 6.8 assists (third best). Being in the top five in both categories is all but unheard-of in pro ball, and now Archibald had done it twice in three years. And even more important, the Kansas City Kings wound up with a 44-38 season record, and made it into the playoffs for the first time in eight years.

Oh — by the way — Archibald was elected to the All-Star team by a nearly unanimous vote.

Speed, Shooting, and Smarts

What makes Nate Archibald a superstar? A friend, his coach, and one of his opponents pretty much agree. It's a very special, very unusual combination of speed, shooting, and smarts. It's Tiny's ability to combine these talents that keeps opponents guessing, and keeps his fans cheering.

"Tiny," says Floyd Lane, who has watched him for nearly 15 years, "is not a 'shooter' the way a Rick Barry or a Bill Bradley is. Tiny is basically a sound ballplayer, and he does everything, all the fundamentals of the game, so well.

"He's so fast that you have to stop his penetration; you have to keep him outside. And you have to play him cautiously, retreating, because if you play him real tight, he'll run right around you, and either lay the ball in or pass it off to a free man."

Kings Coach Phil Johnson, youngest coach in the NBA and 1974-'75 Coach of the Year, agrees that Tiny's penetration — his ability to drive through the middle of the court to bring the ball close to the basket — is his strongest asset. But he points to other skills as well.

"Tiny has developed a fine outside shot," Johnson says, "so the other team can't just play him to drive. Because

if they stay too far back, Tiny will just shoot over them. But what constantly amazes me is his total command of the court. I've seen situations where Tiny will be bringing the ball downcourt, the defense is retreating, flowing back and forth across the court, and suddenly Tiny will see an opening and — snap! — the ball is in the hands of an open man for an easy two points. And very often the man who scores the basket didn't even realize he was free — but Tiny did."

This ability — what Floyd Lane calls Tiny's "fantastic command of the court" — is part of Archibald's special skill. Many guards these days — in fact, most guards who play pro ball — are good shooters. They have to be, to survive in a sport where a big man plays close to the basket and the smaller guards play outside. Also, many guards are quick, because it's part of their job to get the ball out of "traffic" — to find openings. But Tiny Archibald is like

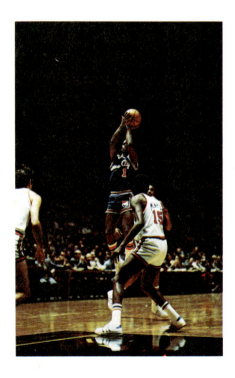

a great piece of Tutti-Frutti gum — there's a little bit of a lot of different flavors in his game.

Speed? There's almost no one faster in the NBA at taking the ball, spotting an opening in the middle of the court, and dribbling through for a layup before anybody else sees what's going on. This speed also makes Archibald very important on the fast break, when a team gets a rebound and, instead of slowly working the ball downcourt, tries to outrun the other team.

"Tiny," says Coach Johnson, "is the best middleman on the break in pro basketball." Tiny's job is to run with the ball down the middle of the court while the forwards sweep down the sides. But when he gets to the free throw line in mid-flight, he has to make a decision: Should he take the ball in himself for a layup? Should he pull up at the free throw line for a shot? Should he pass to one of his teammates who might be in a better position? These decisions have to be made in an instant; a second or two at most. Tiny Archibald knows how to choose the right move even when he is running full speed.

But speed is not the only quality that makes Archibald so effective. He also has great body control. Paul Westphal, who is now with the Phoenix Suns after being traded from the Boston Celtics, describes what this means:

"A lot of guards have quickness, and can move to the basket," he says. "But once they start driving, they're committed to finishing the shot. Tiny has almost total control of his body. He can go at almost full speed, and then change the direction of the play right in the middle of his drive. Very few players have that ability."

Watching Tiny play, the words of Coach Johnson and Paul Westphal come alive. There is Archibald, holding the ball, dribbling, and suddenly he sees a tiny opening between the players. He is off, speeding up from a standing start, almost seeming to go *under* the legs of the much bigger men. Once he is past the player who is supposed to be guarding him, the other team is faced with a very unpleasant choice. They can't just let him go to the basket, because Tiny will simply soar up into the air and score an easy two points. So, usually, another opponent will come over and try to stop Archibald, or, as they say in basketball, he will "drop off" the man he is guarding and try to put himself between Archibald and the basket.

But, of course, that leaves another member of the Kings free; and what Westphal means by "total control of his body" is Tiny's ability to spot an open teammate in the middle of his drive to the basket. When two or three opponents close in on Archibald, instead of trying to complete his shot, Tiny simply zips the ball to a fellow King for an "uncontested" basket — uncontested because the players guarding the other Kings have left them to try to stop Tiny.

To play this way, Tiny needs another attribute described by Johnson in one simple word: "courage." At six feet (some teammates and opponents insist that Tiny is really less than that), Tiny might be expected to stay well outside the basket, relying on his outside shot and passing and ball-handling ability to make the plays. By penetrating into the part of the court where the seven-foot centers play, Tiny knows he is going to get knocked down a lot. "They say basketball is a non-contact sport," Tiny says with a smile, "but that isn't the way it's played here."

Any time a player on one team goes up for a shot near the basket, and the other team's big men try to block the shot or the drive, there is going to be contact, and plenty of it. And when one of the players is about six feet tall, and one of the other players is a foot or so taller, the little guy is the one likely to be knocked to the floor.

But, as Tiny once said, he plays only one way, "fast and

aggressive." All of the injuries, scrapes, and floor burns have not made him change his style. That means points and assists for Archibald, a potent offense for the Kansas City Kings, and headaches for the opposition. When Coach Johnson was asked how he would stop Archibald on defense, he grinned and said, "The first thing I'd do is pray a lot."

On defense, Tiny's size is definitely a disadvantage. "You can't be Tiny's size and really be a great defensive player," says one NBA player. "It's just expecting too much." With a rare exception like Houston's Calvin Murphy, Tiny is always going to be giving away height and size; with the bigger guards like the Knicks' Walt Frazier and the Bullets' Phil Chenier, he's giving away five or six inches. His speed still enables him to be competitive, because he can "play up" against these men — that is, guard them very tightly and pressure them when they try to shoot from outside. He's fast enough to stay with any guard in the league who tries to drive around him.

Still, Tiny is obviously under a handicap on defense for two reasons. First, when a much taller man "takes him low," or down close to the basket, it's hard for Archibald to fight against a pass thrown over his head to a taller opponent. Second, one of the most common offensive tactics in basketball is the "pick." In a "pick," a big man — the center or a forward — stands stock still while a team-mate dribbles the ball close by him. The man guarding the dribbler is then "picked off" by the big man; blocked from following his man. A big, strong guard can try to fight through the pick and stay with his man. If he can't, his only hope is to stay with the big man and let a teammate follow the man with the ball (this is called "switching off"). You can probably guess the problem. When a man of Tiny's size switches, the Kings have a six-foot guard trying to defend against a six-foot-ten or seven-foot opponent, and usually that doesn't work too well. Still, say Tiny's teammates, his quickness and brains make up for most of it.

Besides, in a funny way, Archibald's brilliance on offense helps him out on defense.

"Usually," says Coach Johnson, "Tiny's man is so worried about what Archibald will do on offense that it breaks his concentration; even when his team has the ball, he has to be thinking about what Tiny did the last time he was on offense, and what he might do again."

Back to South Bronx

When a person from a poor background suddenly finds himself a superstar; suddenly finds himself with more money than he ever dreamed of having, it can do strange things to his head. Some athletes almost become drunk on money, the way some people become drunk on liquor or high on drugs. The wealth and what it can buy — the fancy clothes, the big cars and homes, the luxuries — can all but rub out the painful memories of what life was like before.

Tiny Archibald is now one of the highest-paid athletes in the history of professional sports. His yearly salary is between $400,000 and $500,000. He has a contract with a sneaker company that pays him a lot of money for the right to use his name and picture on their advertisements. He has moved his mother and younger brothers and sisters out of the South Bronx to a good home in Roosevelt, Long Island. He lives in a townhouse in a suburb of Kansas City with one of his brothers, who is now settling down after some rough times in the South Bronx.

But unlike so many other people who suddenly become rich, Tiny Archibald has never forgotten where he came from, or the kids who are still there, living through what he lived through until a few short years ago. And as much as any

superstar, he is spending his time working to help these kids fight their way out of poverty.

With all of his money, Tiny could spend his vacations living like a king. Instead, he spends his free time back in the grim neighborhood of the South Bronx. Summer after summer, Archibald is on those streets, in the playgrounds and community centers, talking to kids, teaching them basketball, trying to give them something they may never have had in their lives: hope.

Tiny's work when he isn't playing is even more impressive and important than the things he does on the basketball court. And for him, a broken playground in a slum neighborhood is a more important place for him to be than the biggest, most glamorous basketball court in New York or Los Angeles.

Above all, Archibald tries to keep the kids in school; to get them to continue their educations. He knows that the dream of basketball stardom is very much in the minds of ghetto kids, but he tries to reach them with some hard facts.

"First of all, I try to talk about the odds against making it in pro ball. It's not something everybody's going to do. There's only a certain percent of the kids, of the people coming out of college, that are going to make the pro teams. So I try to tell the kids to get involved in community activities, get some interest in their lives that's going to help them, and that they're going to enjoy for the rest of their lives. I know kids want to be Julius Erving or whoever, but you have to have something else you want to do with your life."

Archibald knows that not every kid will get the message — especially after the signing of three high school stars right into the professional ranks in the last two years. But again, he is very frank in trying to explain the facts to dropout-minded youngsters hoping to become Moses Malones.

"That works only for the big man," he says. "Suppose all you wanted to do was play pro ball. If you were seven feet, or six-feet-ten, like Malone or Daryl Dawkins, then you'd get exposure and everybody would be after you. It'd be much harder for a smaller kid to go right to the pros. You need exposure, and I don't think they can get it from high school. They're going to have to go to college to get that exposure." Archibald speaks from personal experience. It wasn't until *after* his last year in college, in a series of All-Star games, that Tiny first showed his full scoring ability.

Archibald knows full well that telling kids something and getting them to believe it are two different things. That's why he insists on honesty.

"You can't tell them one thing and do another," he says. "You can't jive the kids. Some guys try that. A guy *tells* the kids to be straight, but later the kids see him outside, drinking wine and smoking a joint. And the next time the

man comes around, you can hear the kids saying, 'I wish he would hurry up and cut this, because I saw him do it.' "

Wherever Tiny goes, there always are kids waiting. "Most of the time after practice," says Coach Johnson, "Tiny will wind up talking to the kids, sharing his time with them. There aren't too many athletes you see doing that."

Tiny remembers the days when he was a subway ride away from Madison Square Garden — but a galaxy away from having the money to buy a ticket. One summer, when he was scheduled to play in a benefit game in the Garden, Tiny got dozens of kids from the streets of New York into the game. "They couldn't afford the ticket," Tiny says, "so I just told the people running that game that if they don't get in, I don't play." They got in. Tiny also constantly asks his teammates for their house seats, so that kids who would otherwise never see an NBA game can get in.

In a very important sense, Tiny Archibald is trying to do for

kids what Floyd Lane did for him. Lane, who is still very much involved with the effort to reach ghetto children through athletics, explains what Tiny and other athletes are trying to tell these youths.

"The kids have to realize that in order to reach their basketball goal, they have to continue their education," Lane says. "In order to get into position for a career, they have to go to school. It's not going to come out of the streets. We have to be interested in the development of a youngster as an individual, not just as a basketball player. There's an obligation all of us have as adults to youngsters. And Tiny can really speak to the kids.

"His size is a source of a lot of inspiration to kids, because he's shown that it can be done; you don't have to be a giant to make it in the pros. And more important, Tiny is *there;* they know he cares, because he's out there every summer, fighting to help the kids."

Archibald is outspoken about the needs of these youngsters, and about fellow players who do not contribute enough of their time.

"A lot of athletes make TV commercials about helping the kids," he says bluntly, "but you don't ever see them out in the neighborhoods working with the kids. We need more doctors and lawyers and players going back to their environment instead of making TV commercials about it — they should be talking to white kids, black kids, Puerto Rican kids about staying in school, doing something with their lives."

If there is one regret that Archibald has about his professional life, it is probably that he is not playing in his home town of New York — not because of the basketball, but because it is his home, where the kids who are still trapped need help.

"If I ever played in New York," he says, "my thing would be

a lot different from the glamorous stuff. I grew up there. My thing would be to program a lot of activity in the community, and try to help the youngsters. What can I say? Floyd helped me . . . . I've been playing the game so long that it doesn't make a difference. I enjoy the game, but my real satisfaction is in going back and saying that I helped a kid do something with his life. I relay the message that was relayed to me, and that's what I get my gratification from."

Of course, most of the kids ask Tiny Archibald about basketball first. And here he has some very specific tips.

"Most of the kids I coach are not going to be seven-foot centers," Tiny says. "They're going to be guards or forwards. The guards in particular I tell to concentrate on their ball handling, dribbling, passing, shooting. Most guards are quarterbacks. They have to learn how to get their teams together, because they handle ine ball 90 percent of the time.

"And a lot of this again goes back to schooling — because I tell the kids to read a lot of books about basketball, get everything they can from the libraries, and study: the crossover dribble; how to pivot. Finally, I tell them they've got to put it down; not on paper, but on the cement or the gym. They've got to try and recognize that they must work on their weaknesses. I might tell a kid after watching him, 'You have to work on your jump shot. You drive too much to the basket, and you need a weapon for when they block the middle on you.' They have to learn to mix up their game."

Clearly, Tiny Archibald is no ordinary basketball player. Not in talent, in achievement, or in his commitment. In fact, it's possible that the athletic career of Nate Archibald will only be the beginning of what he will accomplish.

"He's definitely coaching timber," says Floyd Lane. "There's absolutely no doubt about that. But he's got not just the knowledge, he's got respect and leadership quality. I could see him going right up the ladder. He has limitless talents; there's just no telling where he could go."

Finally, as Floyd Lane looks back 15 years to a shy 12-year-old who first came into the P.S. 18 Community Center, and then to the articulate, confident superstar who now captains a contending pro team, a thought strikes him about the man called Tiny, and he smiles with delight.

"He constantly grows," says Lane — "and I don't mean his size."